AF228685

# The History of Transportation

by Chris Oxlade

capstone

To contact Capstone Global Library please call 800-747-4992, or visit our website www.mycapstone.com



Edited by Helen Cox Cannons
Designed by Philippa Jenkins
Picture research by Svetlana Zhurkin
Production by Steve Walker
Originated by Capstone Global Library Ltd

**Library of Congress Cataloging-in-Publication Data**
Library of Congress Cataloging-in-Publication data is available on the Library of Congress website.
ISBN 978 1 4846 4038 8 (hardback)
ISBN 978 1 4846 4042 5 (paperback)
ISBN 978 1 4846 4046 3 (eBook)

*This book has been officially leveled by using the F&P Text Level Gradient ™ Leveling System*

**Acknowledgments**
We would like to thank the following for permission to reproduce photographs: Alamy: Sueddeutsche Zeitung Photo, 22; Dreamstime: Marilyn Gould, cover (left); iStockphoto: BernardAllum, 12; Library of Congress, 21; NASA, 25, 29; National Geographic Creative: H.M. Herget, 10; Newscom: akg-images, 17, 18, 19, 20, Design Pics, 8, Heritage Images/London Metropolitan Archives, 16, Heritage Images/Werner Forman Archive, 6, Hilary Jane Morgan, 11, Mirrorpix, 15, Mirrorpix/Arthur Sidey, 23, picture-alliance/dpa/ Andrej Sokolow, 28, Polaris/Solar Impulse/Rezo/Jean Revillard, 27, Universal Images Group/G. Dagli Orti/ De Agostini, 9, World History Archive, 13; Shutterstock: Everett Collection, 14, IM_photo, 5, Jeffrey B. Banke, 7, K_Boonnitrod, 4, Michael Shake, 1, Nerthuz, cover (right), Pavel L Photo and Video, 26, wws001, 24.

We would like to thank Matthew Anniss for his help in the preparation of this book.

Every effort has been made to contact copyright holders of any material reproduced in this book. Any omissions will be rectified in subsequent printings if notice is given to the publisher.

All the Internet addresses (URLs) given in this book were valid at the time of going to press. However, due to the dynamic nature of the Internet, some addresses may have changed, or sites may have changed or ceased to exist since publication. While the author and publisher regret any inconvenience this may cause readers, no responsibility for any such changes can be accepted by either the author or the publisher.

Printed and Bound in China
PO4603

# Table of Contents



Some words are shown in bold, **like this**. You can find out what they mean by looking in the glossary.

Thousands of years ago, during the Stone Age, most people in the world did not travel far from home. There were no cars or bicycles and no roads. People might have walked along a path to the next village.

People learned to train animals such as yaks to carry packs about 6,000 years ago.

Since the Stone Age, there have been many
new inventions. They have made transportation
easier and faster. We can now travel easily
between towns and cities. We can even travel
halfway around the world in a day in airplanes.

# Wheels and Carts

The wheel was invented in about 3500 BC. The first wheels were made of planks joined edge to edge. A simple two-wheeled cart could carry a lot more on it than an animal could carry on its back.

This work of art was made in 2500 BC. It shows Sumerians using a cart with an early version of wheels.

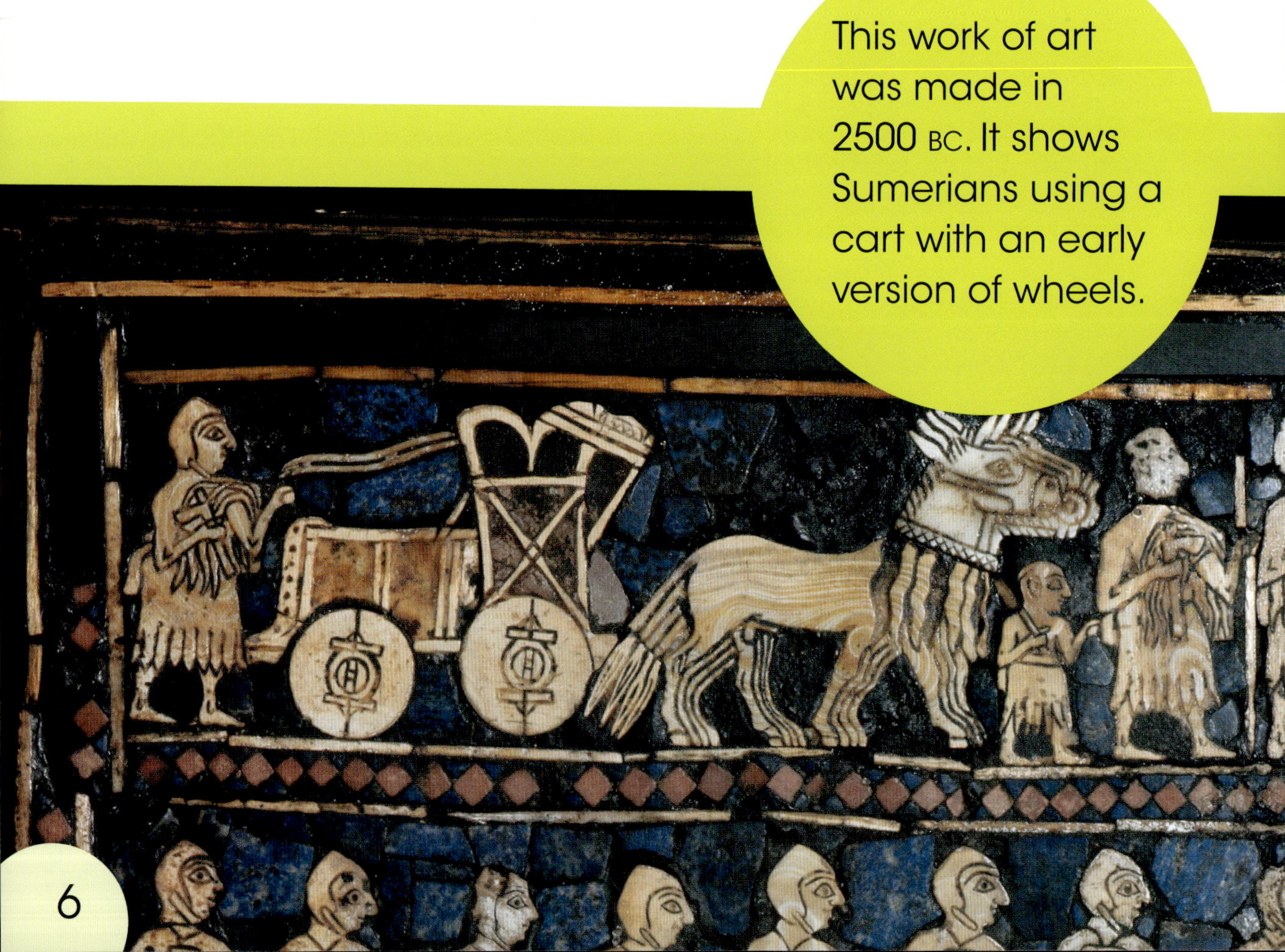

Wheels with **spokes** were invented in about 2000 BC. Spoked wheels were lighter and stronger than solid wheels. Hundreds of years later, the ancient Romans began building roads paved with stone. This made travel across their huge **empire** easier.

People may have gone to sea on rafts made from logs or **reeds** as long as 40,000 years ago. The oldest boats ever found are from around 10,000 years ago. They were dugout canoes made out of tree trunks.

Dugout canoes were made by burning away wood to make a hollow.

People simply paddled their boats
until sails were invented in about
3100 BC. The first known sailing boats traveled
on the River Nile in Egypt. Their square sails
were raised up to catch the wind.

Around the world, craftsmen slowly learned how to build bigger, stronger, and faster ships. Most ships had a **hull** of wooden planks over a wooden frame. **Cargo** such as **grain**, wine, and oil were loaded on board.

The ancient Greeks traded goods around their empire.

Explorers sailed across the oceans to explore new land. Some went to claim new land as their own. New inventions such as the **rudder** made long journeys by sea much easier.

During the 1800s, engineers in Europe and the United States dug hundreds of miles of canals. Barges carried **cargo** such as coal or dry foods along the canals between cities, ports, and factories. A barge could carry more than a wagon on a road.

This illustration from 1828 shows barges carrying cargo along a London canal.

Crowds went to see the first passengers on the Stockton and Darlington railroad.

In 1825, the world's first passenger railroad started running. It was called the Stockton and Darlington Railway. Passenger coaches were pulled along by horses, then later by steam-powered **locomotives**. The first underground railroad opened in London in 1863.

# Steamships

By the end of the 1700s, steam-powered ships began to take over from sailing ships. Steam engines turned paddle wheels or propellers in the water. Steamships were easily faster than sailing ships because they did not need wind to power them.

In 1819, *Savannah* became the first steamship to cross the Atlantic Ocean.

French liner
SS *Normandie*
was the fastest
liner of its time.

Shipbuilders began building steamships
with metal instead of wood. By the 1930s, huge
steam-powered liners were carrying people
around the world. The biggest and fastest liners
sailed across the Atlantic Ocean between
Europe and the U.S.

In 1817, German engineer Karl Drais invented a heavy wooden bicycle with no pedals. It was known as a **draisienne**. In 1885, the first modern-looking bicycle was built. It was the Rover Safety bicycle.

A rider moved a **draisienne** along by pushing his or her feet against the ground.

In 1869, Frenchman Ernest Michaux put a small steam engine on a bicycle. Then, in 1885, Gottlieb Daimler built a motorcycle with a gas engine. Within a few years, motorcycles were popular across Europe and the U.S.

The word "car" possibly comes from the Romans. The Latin word *carrus* means "wheeled vehicle." The first cars of the 1800s were horse-drawn carriages with engines. German inventors Karl Benz and Gottlieb Daimler built two of the very first cars in 1885 and 1886.

Karl Benz built this car in 1885.

Before long, there were lots of small car-making factories. But these cars were very expensive. Then, in 1908, the Ford Motor Company started making their Model T car. It was small, cheap, and easy to look after.

In 1783, a human took off in a flying machine for the first time. The machine was a hot air balloon. It was built in France by the Montgolfier brothers. About 100 years later, people began to travel in giant gas-filled airships.

Between 1928 and 1937, the Graf Zeppelin airship took thousands of people across the Atlantic Ocean.

American brothers Orville and Wilbur Wright
made history in 1903. They built the first
successful powered airplane. It was called the
*Flyer*. The *Flyer's* first flight lasted just 12 seconds.
Many other inventors soon took to the air.

# Bigger and Faster Planes

By the end of World War I (1914–1918), there were large bomber aircraft. Some of these bombers were turned into planes to carry passengers. These were the first airliners. Airliners got larger, faster, and more comfortable through the 1920s and 1930s.

The *Boeing 314 Clipper* was a flying boat that landed on water.

The giant *Boeing 747* airliner made its first flight in 1970.

The jet engine was a very important invention in the history of air transportation. It allowed aircraft to fly much faster and higher than before. The first jet fighter planes flew in 1939. By the 1950s, big jet airliners were taking off.

Rockets are machines that transport spacecraft into space. Rockets were developed in the 1920s and 1930s. By the 1960s, rockets were carrying astronauts onboard spacecraft into space.

Soviet **cosmonaut** Yuri Gagarin went into space in 1961, on board a Vostok spacecraft.

Armstrong and Aldrin landed on the moon in this lunar module.

In 1969, two American astronauts, Neil Armstrong and Buzz Aldrin, landed on the moon. They traveled there with Michael Collins in the *Apollo 11* spacecraft. Another spacecraft, the *Space Shuttle*, made dozens of trips to space between 1981 and 2011.

Types of fuel in engines include gasoline and **diesel**. These engines give out gases that **pollute** the air. In the 1990s, **hybrid** cars and electric cars were developed. Electric cars do not pollute the air.

Electric cars must be **recharged** when their batteries run down.

Engineers are now making solar powered cars, boats, and planes. This means they have solar panels that capture light from the sun. The vehicles then turn the light into electricity to power their electric motors.

# Future Transportation

What new forms of transportation will we see in the near future? Driverless cars are already being tested and driverless taxis are being used in Pittsburgh, Pennsylvania. The car drives itself. It finds its way from place to place by computer. We could all be using driverless cars one day.

This is a driverless car being tested by Google.

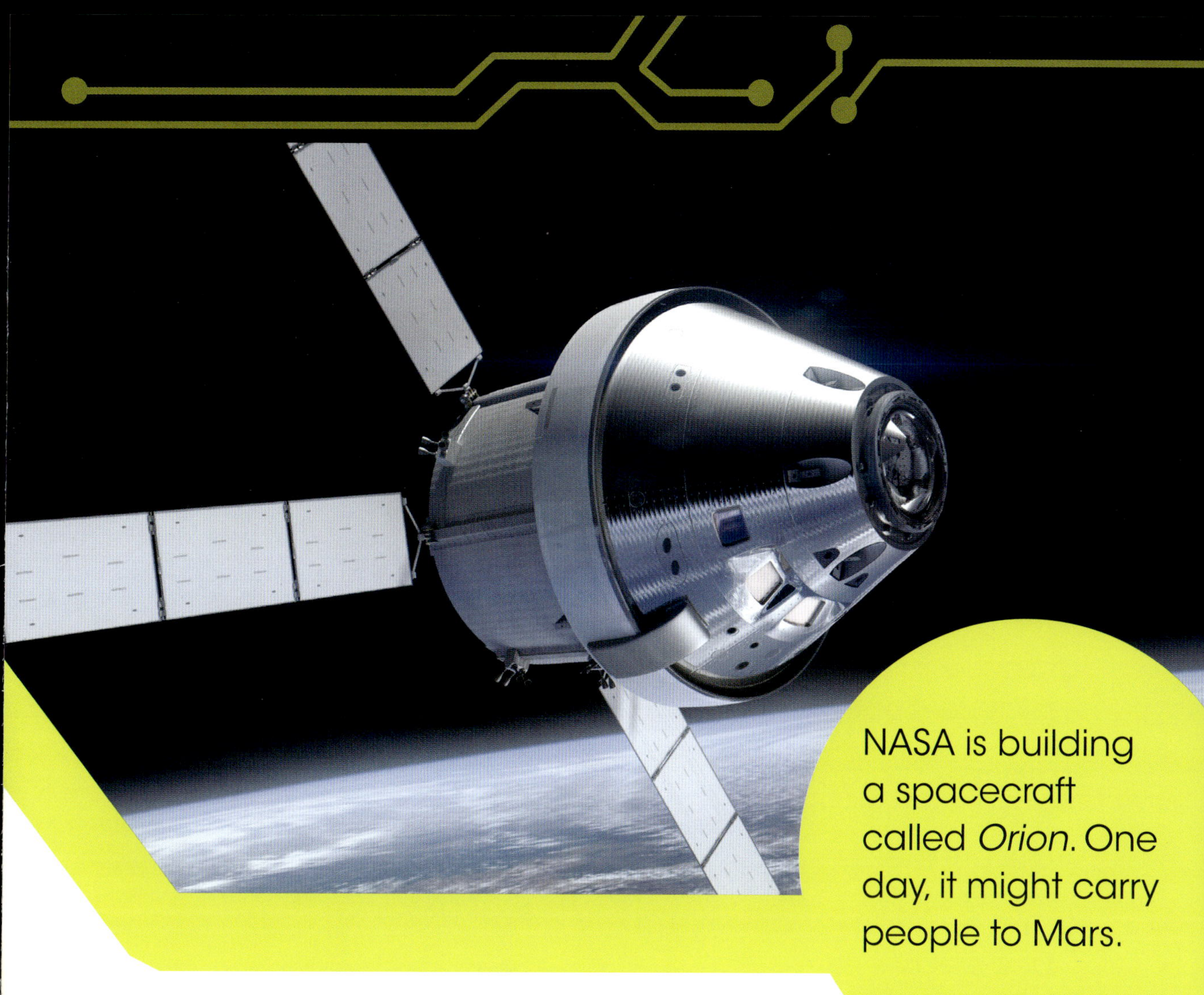

NASA is building a spacecraft called *Orion*. One day, it might carry people to Mars.

In the air, **drones** and giant airships may start carrying **cargo**. Engineers are designing new spacecraft. They hope these spacecraft will one day carry astronauts and all their food and equipment to Mars.

**cargo**—goods carried on a ship or other vehicle

**carrack**—a medieval sailing ship with three or four masts

**cosmonaut**—a Russian astronaut

**diesel**—a type of fuel used in many vehicle engines

**drone**—an unmanned, remote-controlled aircraft

**empire**—a group of countries ruled by a single person or government

**grain**—wheat, or other type of cereal

**hull**—the main body of a ship, which makes it float

**hybrid**—a car that has both an electric motor and an engine that uses fuel

**linen**—a type of cloth similar to cotton

**locomotive**—railroad engine

**papyrus**—material made from papyrus, which is a water plant

**pollute**—to put harmful or dangerous chemicals into the environment

**propeller**—a device with spinning blades that help a ship or airplane move

**recharge**—to put electricity into a battery, so the battery can be used again

**reed**—a plant with tall leaves that grows in water or on wet ground

**rudder**—a flat handle at the back of a boat used for steering

**spoke**—a rod that joins the center of a wheel to the rim of a wheel

## Read More

Davis, Lynn. *Henry Ford.* Amazing Inventors & Innovators. Minneapolis: Abdo Publishing, 2016.

Peterson, Megan Cooley. *The First Airplanes.* Famous Firsts. North Mankato, Minn.: Capstone Press, 2015

Simons, Lisa M. Bolt. *Transportation Long Ago and Today.* Long Ago and Today. North Mankato, Minn.: Capstone Press, 2015.

## Internet Sites

FactHound offers a safe, fun way to find Internet sites related to this book. All of the sites on FactHound have been researched by our staff.

Here's all you do:

Visit *www.facthound.com*

Type in this code: 9781484640388